GRANITE
The Bullmastiff Story

Louise Chadborne

ISBN: 978-1-7350328-3-2

Age Audience: K-Fourth grade (5 years old-10 years old)

Printed in the United States of America

T. Fielding-Lowe Company, Publisher

https://www.tfieldinglowecompany.com

This book is dedicated to all those up in heaven looking down, smiling, and slobbering.

This book belongs to

_____

Follow the paw prints!

My name is Granite and this is my story. I was born in Chepachet, Rhode Island, not far from the Massachusetts border, on March 5th. My mommy and daddy were pure breeds. That means they were a queen and king in the doggie world. They come from a long line of bullmastiffs.

Bullmastiffs are guardians. They protect people. Protecting people is so important that mommy and daddy were given special papers. On my paper, it said that my last name is Applehill. If I looked up my name, I would find my family members located all around the world. On each of our papers, they would say that we are pure bullmastiffs.

I weighed 8 pounds when I was born. It is important to know how much a puppy weighs and how old they are before going to their new home.

My new home is going to be with my paw parent, Louise. Do you have a picture of yourself when you were a baby?

When my new mommy, Louise, came to see us. My parents got so excited that they jumped on her. Their bodies were as tall as she was standing on their hind legs. They gave her big kisses. Just like I did!

I was born along with seven sisters and brothers. All my sisters and brothers, including myself, wore different colored ribbons tied around our necks so that our new paw parents could tell us apart.

Some of us looked orange, and some of us looked tan. What color was your hair when you were born? The bullmastiff's color of fur can be brindle, fawn, and red. Brindle is the color of a tiger's fur. Fawn is the color of a lion's fur. Red is the color of a foxes' fur.

Brindle

Fawn

Red

My sisters, brothers, and I all got along most of the time. However, some would try to push into mommy for more milk, or at times we would fight over the same toy until one of us would give up or grab a different toy. We had to learn to share and get along. They call that "socializing" in doggie talk.

I do not remember how I was chosen from my litter. Other than my new mommy saying, "I did my homework on this type of breed, the bullmastiff. I LOVE this breed of dog. I WILL give this baby boy a VERY GOOD home. He will have toys and go for rides. I WILL CARE for him, FEED him, bathe him, and take him to the doggie doctor. But, most importantly, LOVE HIM ALWAYS. He will be part of our family. He will have a mommy, daddy, and big brother".

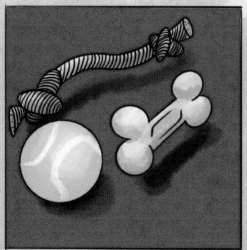

I was still too small to leave my doggie mommy and daddy. I was just a few weeks old. My paw parents made calls every week to determine my progress, such as eating, gaining weight, and walking.

Also, they were sent pictures of me. I looked so cute in those pictures, even prettier in person when my new family would visit me. My new family took turns picking me up carefully. We would kiss and hug each other. They loved giving me belly rubs, and I liked getting them.

Finally, I was eight weeks old! This meant that I would say goodbye to my mommy, daddy, and seven brothers and sisters to start a NEW life in Dudley, Massachusetts.

When I arrived at my new home, there was a party. Guess who was the guest of honor? Me!

During the party, I was given my new name by mommy, daddy, and big brother. Are you ready? My new name is Granite. Whenever they would call my name, I would come to them.

The party was fun. I received all kinds of toys, a new bed, treats, and a very big crate that my mommy called a condo. It was that big!

Right away, my training began. I learned how to sit, stay, down and give my paw. It was hard for me to "come" on command.

I hated being stuck in one place. I would get loose by breaking free from my chain, lifting the fence gate's handle, and pushing open the door. I did this a lot. I enjoyed my freedom and would run all over my neighborhood.

I remember one morning when I was a few years old. My mommy was dressed for work. Work helps pay for my treats/food, so I am okay that she needs to leave me five days a week for work.

Oh, back to my story. There was morning dew on our grass. I had seen our neighbor way down at the other end of a street. Before my mommy saw him, l started to run over to him to say hi.

I forgot my mommy was holding on to the other end of the leash. I started to run and began picking up speed. I weighed over 120 pounds; it looked like mommy was water skiing across the front lawn with her high-heeled shoes. While passing the side of our house, mommy tried to grab the corner to hang on. I was so strong that mom had to let go of the leash.

When I got to my neighbor, he was dressed in his police uniform. I thought I was going to doggie jail. Instead, he said, "hi Granite!"

I gave him his good morning kiss. Mommy approached and said that she was sorry. All was forgiven. Maybe not all. I did not get my morning treat! Has that ever happened to you? Maybe your mommy, daddy, or someone you were with decided you misbehaved, and you did not earn a sticker, prize, or a treat.

In my new family, I only had one big brother. His name is Jarrid. Jarrid loved me so much, and so did all his friends.

Jarrid, his friends, and I were huge sports fans. Jarrid would put his sports jersey on me, and we all would play football together in the front yard.

Sometimes Jarrid's friends would spend the night, and I would sleep on top of them. Just like my other family in Chepachet. All of us snored into the early morning.

I grew from a small puppy to a very big and strong dog weighing 150-165 pounds. I was all muscle with a huge head and neck to match the rest of my body. People would look at me and be scared! At times, I would look at them and think the same thing. Woof! Woof!

Also, did I tell you that I drooled a lot? When it was food time, I would be so excited to eat that drool would come down my jowls and form puddles on the floor. When I would shake my head, lookout! My drool would fly everywhere! My parents were always trying to wipe my mouth or jowl like I was a baby spitting up.

I was also a perfect guard dog. I would not bark much. Instead, I would sit, listen, and wait in the dark. I liked the darkness because it allowed me to use my senses to protect my family; however, because my size was so BIG, people would not mess with my family or me. I loved my family and always would protect them!

I love riding in cars. Do you? We would visit my grandmother and two grandfathers, along with other family members. Who do you like to visit?

On the way, we stopped for ice cream with the cows in Charlton, Massachusetts. No chocolate, though. Chocolate is not healthy for dogs to eat. It makes us sick, so instead I was able to have vanilla.

"Those cows are bigger than me," I remember thinking. "I hope they don't try to take my ice cream." When I got my vanilla ice cream, I ate it fast with my big tongue. It was so yummy!

On another day, mom and I went to the Webster Post Office. I rode in the back of her blue blazer. Folks kept looking at me as they passed by the car while mom was inside. I guess they never saw a big dog before, like me. They would see me and would walk further away from the blazer.

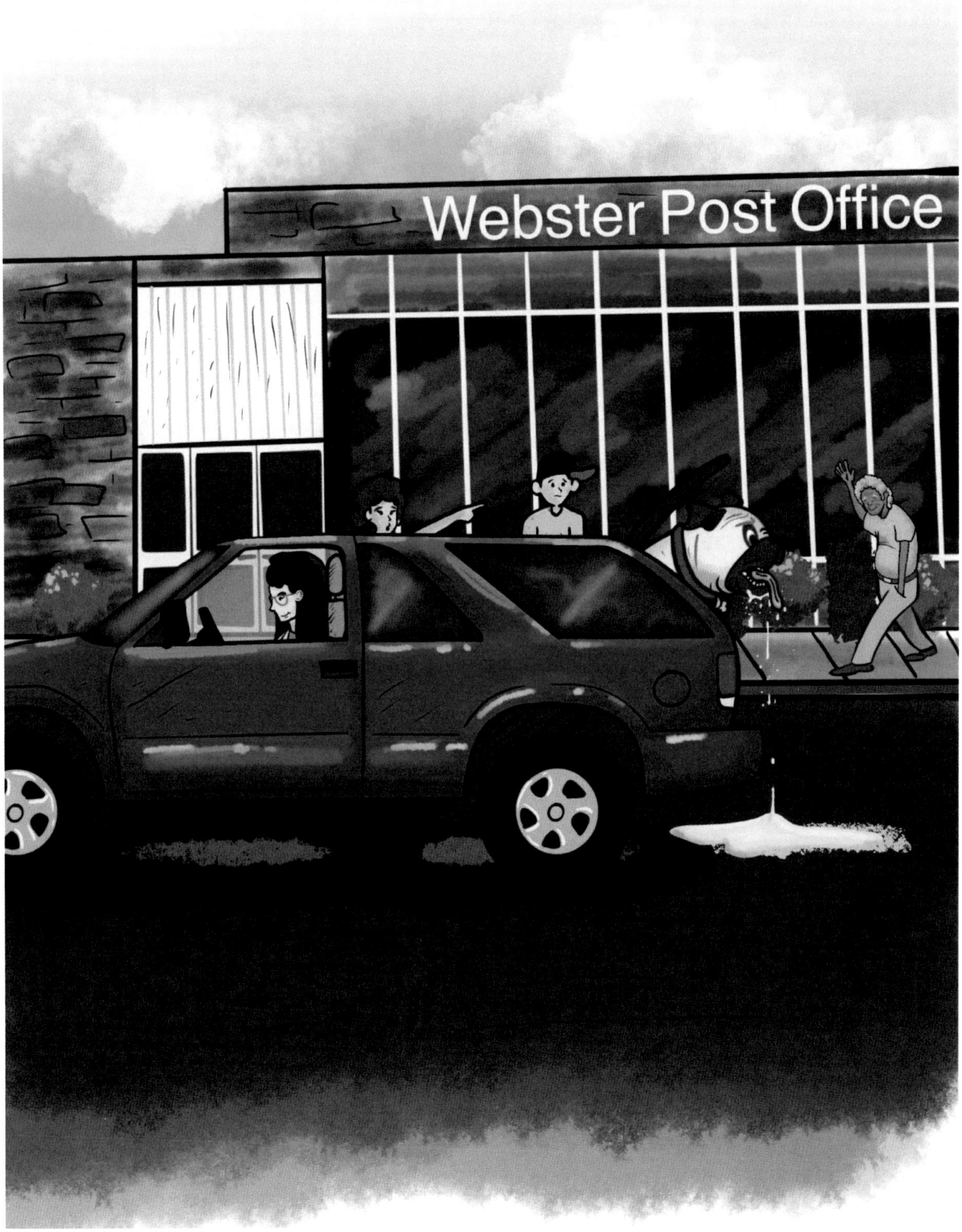
Webster Post Office

While I waited for mom to come out of the post office, one of my favorite grandfathers got out of his car and came over to me. People were watching us and must have been thinking, "what in the world is this guy doing. This big dog is going to gobble him up". But instead, grandfather reached into the car and began petting and talking to me.

What they did not know is that we were family. Of course, he had some treats that he gave me too! "Hi there, Granite! How are you?" said grandpa. "Where is Mom?" I gave him so many kisses. He was laughing, and folks just stared. Isn't that funny?!

You should also know that I helped with chores around the house and yard. Bullmastiffs are a working breed-type of dog. That means I must stay busy to keep my brain sharp. Like when you have homework to do to make good grades. Dogs love to learn too!

My favorite chore to do around the house is raking the backyard. Here is a picture of me. What chores do you do at home?

I love my family. I have to go now and help out around my house because I want a special treat. Maybe mom will give me a giant bone. Enjoy spending time with your family as I do. I will bark at you later.

Pet Tips!

- ☐ LOVE THEM ALWAYS

- ☐ GIVE THEM CLEAN WATER AND FOOD ACCORDING TO THEIR MEAL SCHEDULE

- ☐ REGULAR VETERINARY APPOINTMENTS, ALONG WITH FLEA, HEARTWORM TREATMENT

- ☐ DAILY WALKS AND PLAYTIME

- ☐ BRUSH THEIR FUR AND TRIM THEIR NAILS

- ☐ POOP SCOOP!

Granite is helping me do yard work. He is raking the backyard.

About the Author

I am Louise Chadborne, and I am the author of *'Granite the Bullmastiff'* which was my first book to land on Amazon and other platforms. An entrepreneur by day, author by night, I aim to bring the flavor of diversity to the vivid canvas through my writings for the entire world to read.

I began writing my debut book to pay tribute to my dear dog Granite, who died and left me emotionally devastated. Through my eloquent writing, I've written this book dedicated to sharing my profound, personal experiences of losing my dog, Granite.

Born and based in Webster, Massachusetts, I worked in the Department of Mental Health for more than 32 years and co-own *Frostys Tree Stand Farm.*

When not writing, I can be found volunteering at the zoo because animals bring me joy and a feeling of companionship. I am also passionate about collecting coins; it may seem like a boring hobby, but trust me, coin collecting is a relaxing hobby you can pursue your entire life.

I believe that books can change the world, so I use my writings to empower and inspire people of all ages. My book has received praise and recognition through multiple platforms. You can catch my writings with a cup of Earl Grey tea or hot coffee.

Made in the USA
Middletown, DE
30 July 2021